This book belongs to

....

....

....

For Hanno, far away and still best friends. Thanx, pardner. –D.B.

David, thanks for being a star! –M.W.

tiger tales

an imprint of ME Media, LLC

202 Old Ridgefield Road, Wilton, CT 06897

Published in the United States 2006

Originally published in Great Britain 2005

By Oxford University Press

Text copyright ©2005 David Bedford

Illustrations copyright ©2005 Melanie Williamson

CIP data is available

ISBN 1-58925-397-3

Printed in Singapore

1 3 5 7 9 10 8 6 4 2

Hound Dog

by David Bedford

Illustrated by

Melanie Williamson

tiger tales

Hound Dog was moving to the country. He would miss the city's streets and houses he knew so well.

But most of all, he would miss his best friend, Jojo.

"Will you write letters?" Jojo asked.

"Every day!" promised Hound Dog.

Hound Dog sent Jojo a letter after his first long day in the country.

WANTED

Mean Dog Gang!

Dear Jojo,
I've meet three dogs: Giblet, Shaker, and Rags. They are called the Mean Dog Gang.
Love, Hound Dog

Jojo wrote right back.

Dear Hound Dog,

A new dog moved into your old house! His name is Zoot. I might see if he wants to play.

Love, Jojo

Hound Dog and Jojo played with their new friends.

Dear Jojo,

Rags said I have to learn how to spit. But the first time I tried, I dribbled on Giblet!

From your best friend, Hound

Jojo
4 Pooch Lane
The City

Dear Best Friend Hound,

Zoot is one of those spotted dogs who can roll a ball with his nose. You would be very good at it, Hound Dog, and I know you would like Zoot.

Love, Jojo

Zoot rolling his new ball

He loves it!

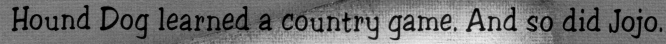

Hound Dog learned a country game. And so did Jojo.

Dear Jojo,

Shaker said if I want to be a Mean Dog, I'll have to learn how to lasso. You'd be the best at it, Jojo. The first time I tried, I lassoed Shaker!

Love from Country Dog Hound

Dear Country Dog Hound,

Is it okay if I show Zoot your letters? He used to live in the country, and he knows all about it. He showed me how to lasso!

Love from Country Dog Jojo!

Hound Dog's new friends weren't always easy to get along with. Sometimes it was easier to write to Jojo.

Dear Jojo,
Giblet said if I want to be his friend, I'll have to chase cats. If I don't, all the Mean Dogs will chase ME! Jojo, what should I do?
Love, Hound-in-Trouble

Dear Hound-in-Trouble,

I showed Zoot your letter and he said, "No way! Chasing cats is mean!" He wants to come and see you.

Love, Jojo

P.S. Don't chase cats and keep writing!

hide our bones

Look at Zoot lasso!

me and Zoot

your letters

Oops!

Hound Dog had nobody else to play with, so in the end, he did what the Mean Dogs wanted.

Dear Jojo and Zoot,
This morning I chased cats with the Mean Dogs. But I only chased one, and it was only a game.
From Mean Dog Hound

Hound Dog didn't EVER mean to catch a cat.
But it wasn't long before...

he did!

my new friend!

Dear Jojo and Zoot,

I caught a cat! I felt REALLY bad.
I said I was sorry and that I was only
pretending to chase her.

Then, guess what? The cat said,
"Let's be friends, Hound Dog!"

Love, Happy Hound

P.S. I don't know what I'm going to do
when the Mean Dogs see my new friend.

The next day, Hound Dog ran out of paper.
But he kept writing on anything he could find.

Look at them run!

Fast!

After Hound Dog's next letter, Jojo and Zoot decided that Hound Dog needed their help.

Dear Jojo and Zoot,

I chased the Mean Dogs away! Then all these other dogs appeared. They'd been hiding from the Mean Dogs all along!

The new dogs have a ball and we all played with it. I tried rolling the ball with my nose, but I think I need more practice.

Love from Hound

P.S. We're really worried that the Mean Dogs will come back!

The Mean Dogs did come back. But Hound Dog was ready for them.

pssssssst

Dear Jojo and Zoot,

When the Mean Dogs came back, they didn't look so mean anymore.

Giblet said, "We want to play, too."

Shaker said, "Our ball's out of air. Rags bit it."

Rags said, "We don't want to be left out. We want to be friends."

The other dogs said they could play as long as they weren't the Mean Dogs anymore.

Love, Hound Dog

P.S. I wish, wish, wish you and Zoot could be here.

Gang. 6

Choooo   Choooo

When Hound Dog went to mail his letter,
he had a big surprise.

"Jojo, you're here! My wish has come true!"
he cried.

Hound Dog and Zoot became fast friends.

"Howdy, Hound Dog," said Zoot.

"Howdy, Zoot," said Hound Dog.

From that day on, the Mean Dogs weren't mean, nobody chased cats, and Hound Dog had a **HOWLING** good time in the country.

Dear Jojo and Zoot,

Please visit your friends in the country again soon. You won't believe what Giblet, Shaker, and Rags are doing now—they're teaching everyone to DANCE!

Love from your very best country friend,
Hound Dog

P.S. Yee-HAWWWWWwwwww!

Careful, Duncan!

Rags with the mice

our gang!

Cheep and me

Rags and me playing

Giblet and Lotto

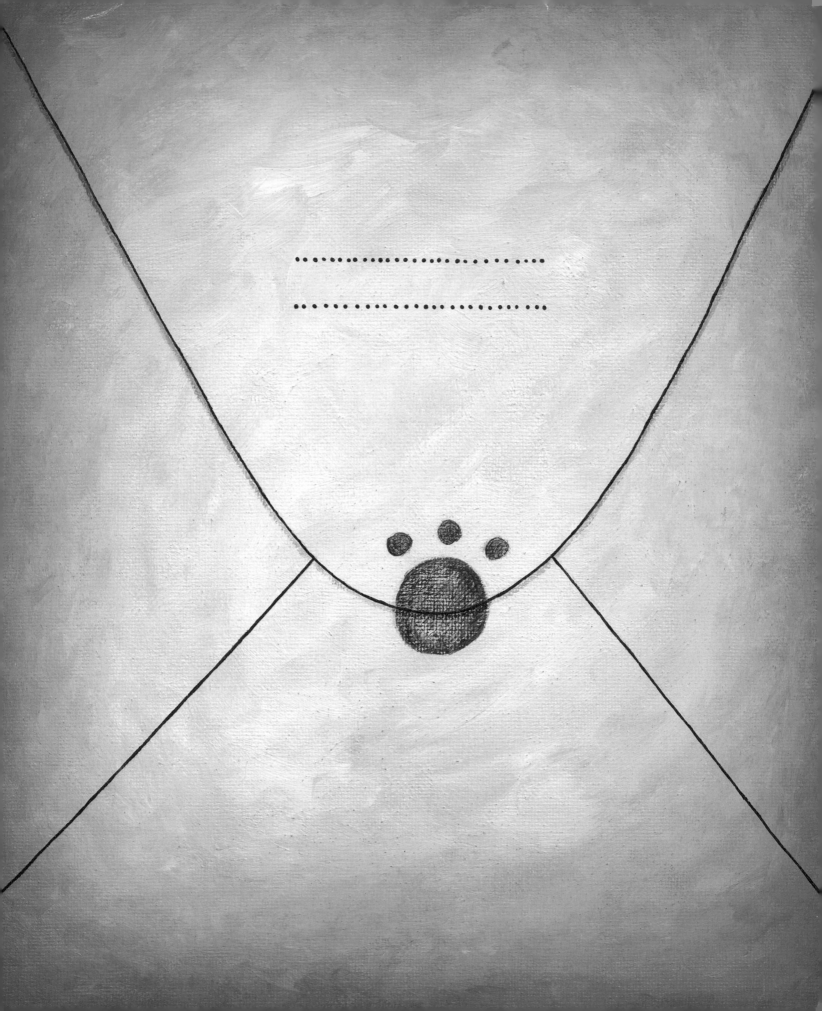